FIRST RAIN

FIRST RAIN

DONNA WEIR-SOLEY

PEEPAL TREE

First published in Great Britain in 2006
Peepal Tree Press Ltd
17 King's Avenue
Leeds LS6 1QS
UK

ISBN 1 84523 033 7

Peepal Tree gratefully acknowledges Arts Council support

ACKNOWLEDGEMENTS

I would like to thank my incredible support system which consists of Mom and Gunny (what would I do without you two?) and my sisters by choice, my children's aunties and godmothers without whose support I could not survive to see this in print: Claudia May, Heather Andrade, Opal Palmer Adisa, Pepper Black. I am constantly overwhelmed by your love and support. Thank you all!

To Kim Lyons, Lorna McCalla, and Jackie and Joel Watson, thanks for loving me and supporting me, regardless.

I want to acknowledge the Mellon Minority Undergraduate Foundation (now Mellon Mays) and the Woodrow Wilson Foundation for their generous support over the years, with special thanks to Sylvia Sheridan, Richard Hope, Lydia English and William Mitchell.

I want to acknowledge the editorial feedback of Opal Palmer Adisa, and Dorothea Smartt, and my colleagues in the writing program at Florida International University Campbell McGrath and Denise Duhamel, all of whom have read some of these poems at various stages of development. I also want to acknowledge Eunice Tate and Carole Boyce Davies who have paid me the compliment of including some of these poems in their collections. Different versions of select poems have also been published in various journals including *MaComere: the Journal of Caribbean Women Writers and Scholars*, *The Caribbean Writer*, The *Carrier Pidgin*, *Frontiers*, et. al. I want to thank Jeremy Poynting and Hannah Bannister for invaluable editorial support.

For someone who was born in a rural working-class environment in Jamaica, such as I was, there were only two ways to advance up the social ladder: education and/or migration. I was fortunate enough to have had access to both, so it would be remiss of me if I did not acknowledge the support of teachers and mentors. At Hunter College of the City University of New York, where I took my first degree, Melinda Goodman, Audre Lorde, Frank Kirkland, Louise DeSalvo, Myrna Bain and Richard Barickman were all unwavering in their support of my academic and literary pursuits. Upon the advisement of the late Audre Lorde, I went from Hunter to the University of California, Berkeley, to pursue graduate degrees. There I met Barbara Christian who, along with

Janet Adelman, encouraged me to continue writing my poetry and to resist the tendency towards academic homogenization that would rob me of my poetic voice. And, to those early teachers who first confirmed that I had something to say, Mrs. Cowan, Mrs. Faulkner and Ms. Rose Salmon (St. Elizabeth Technical High School, Jamaica) and Perry Weiner and Judy Rosenbaum (Andrew Jackson High, Queens, New York), I'm not sure I would have made it past high school without that knowledge, so thank you for the part you played in helping me survive my youth with integrity, with my dreams intact.

And to my colleagues at Florida International University who have supported my decision to continue writing and publishing poetry, especially my brilliant colleague and trusted confidante, Heather Andrade, internationally recognised linguist Tometro Hopkins, acclaimed poets Campbell McGrath and Denise Duhamel, and prolific Jewish Studies scholar Meri-Jane Rochelson, thank you for understanding the continuity between the poetry I write and the migration stories we teach.

A big shout-out to Carolyn Cooper, who champions all ragamuffins, including the reformed ones like me! Thank you for your consistent support of my scholarly work and my poetry.

And to my family members who have prayed me over: Curene, Judene, Chloe, Ricky, Claudia, Morette, Mom, Loris, and those who are praying without me knowing, thank you, your prayers mean everything, your prayers move everything, keep them coming...

To my sisters and brothers, you are the inspiration for so many of these poems... I hope you enjoy them.

To my husband Cush and my children Jedhi, Iyah and Kai, thanks for putting up with me through all the ups and downs. I love you all.

To my children, my nieces and nephews, my cousins, and their children and to all my students, *First Rain* is part of my legacy to you.

And last, but by no means least, to Professor Houston Baker, whose incredible support and encouragement has helped me to understand the relevance of this work to the literary tradition of the Black diaspora, as well as to the broader academic and non-academic community, thank you. You are filling a void, left by my brilliant but sadly, too-soon-departed mentors, that is greater than you will ever know...

I want to give thanks and praise to the Almighty God, who gives me breath, health, strength and inspiration to keep going against all the odds and because He has not given me the spirit of fear, but of power and of love and of a sound mind.

First Rain is dedicated to my grandparents, Theresa Matilda McCalla and Knollis McCalla and to my mother Daisy McCalla and my father Kenneth Weir. And, to Louise Bennett, who taught me to be proud of my heritage, long before it was fashionable.

CONTENTS

BUSH ROOTS

ROOTS

I come from hard-packed red dirt
yielding coffee, cocoa, pimento, butter ackees and soft white yam
(bright white and sweet like the smile of my first boyfriend).

I come from hardworking
tough-loving, tenderhearted dark men
and tall, statuesque healer women,
midwives, priestesses, dreamers and seer women
with skin shades ranging from
common mango yellow to
blue-black star-apple purple.

I am packed hard, impervious,
softly yielding fruit in and out of season,
like the earth that nurtured me.

BUSH MAGIC

I am the product of:
my grandfather's dutty-tuff vision
my grandmother's castor-oil boiling,
baby-birthing, life-sustaining bush magic
my uncle's soft-spoken, iron-clad love
my auntie's fine midnight stitches
my mother's nightly dream-weaving
my daddy's coal-skill burning,
rock-stone breaking, machete-wielding
three-finger-jack history of strength,
courage and endurance
and the thing that can break me
has not yet been invented.

TERESA MATILDA MCCALLA MCCALLA

To feel the weight of a loss that ungrounds you
and yet not know its source, is a cruelty
only human memory could design.

For years I felt adrift from my moorings,
without compass in uncharted waters
never really understanding why,
until I took a train from Oxford to Sheffield
to find you waiting on a mantelpiece
in Uncle Brisente's living room,
your oval face nicely framed in silver,
skin tinged a reddish-bronze glow,
warm and fragrant like pimento.
In your floral skirt and crisp round-collar white blouse,
your long bony hands crossed in your lap,
you could have been dressed for a Wednesday-night prayer meeting.
Grandma, your eyes held the high purple of the St. Catherine hills,
and the promise of rain water.

I brought your picture back to New York with me
to copy and distribute to the family
who were losing you, Mummah, bit by precious bit.

The first night back you dreamt me
red overripe coffee beans.
I woke up smelling their sickly-sweet aroma
feeling the damp earth of the coffee walk
and hearing the chick-man-chicks singing in the pear tree.

You said you were tired,
had been picking pimento in Fustick Hill
and gathering coffee from Breeze Mill,
asked me to pick the red, pity-me-lickle ants from your skin,
rub your feet with bay rum.

15

You were harvesting your crops to save
for Bertina's plane ticket to America,
Brisente's passage to England,
and no, you couldn't stop to rest or talk with me
because, didn't I see, there was so much work to be done,
the gungo peas not yet on the fire for dinner
And what would Mass Knoll say
when he come back from the fields
and no dinner nuh ready?

So I walked with you to the dirt-floor kitchen
and swept the fire hearth while you gathered firewood.
I watched your eyes redden from the smoke
as you blew into the brushwood to get the fire started
and sat back, coughing, as tiny flames leapt up
devouring the brushwood and igniting the logs
under your three-legged dutch pot.

When your pot was bubbling with green gungo peas,
salt beef, white flour dumplings and soft white yam
you filled your clay pipe with plug tobacco
and lit it. Turning the bowl inside your mouth,
you rocked back on your heels in the hard-packed dirt,
your long floral skirt fanning out round you,
rings of smoke forming around your head
and said

Lissen good:
Ah was born Teresa Matilda Touban,
but evvy badda call mi Miss Mattie or Sistah Mattie
Mi madda was a Maroon, fighter people dem
she was a healer an a midwife;
Mi daddy people dem come from India
im come ere wen im a bway
an start cut sugar cane from im inna short pants.
Mi daddy had a wandring spirit

couldn't sit one place fe long
Mi Madda, she know all a de ole African ways
Some she teach me, some me feget
but de herbs business stick wid me.

Mi nevah have a easy life
Mi born inna struggle
Mi birth thirteen pickney;
one born dead
one get poliomylitis from im a baby
one get a bad injection almost cripple im.
Mi bury two husband
Cousin dem, same name,
one jetblack and cool like de stone in im water jar
de odder one red like wite people,
eye dem green like de pickney dem glass marble.
Dem did love me, de two a dem, inna dem way,
but de fus one cubbitch and prideful,
never could forgive im people dem,
who tun dem back wen im married me
Never did forgive me fe being de reason.
De todder one cross, and got a wandrin spirit,
like mi daddy. Couldn't settle down,
walk out all de lan im buy and
de res wat im come find me wid,
never fine de peace im a walk a look fah.

Sun never ketch me inna bed
so me no know wha sunlight
feel like thru de window inna yuh face,
but me know bout donkey pad-up wid clothes
fe go a river before day bruk Monday morning,
an me know bout holding de head
of somebody you love in you lap
till de last breath leave dem body
and watching you pickney dem catch plane and ship,

17

one by one, two by two, gawn a foreign
an you don't know if you will live to see dem
come back home again.

Dese same hands help birth plenty grands into dis world,
plait plenty hair, and ease a dying woman from de heaviness
of stillbirth when de doctors give she over fe dead —
de same oman who never talk to me again
after she find out she couldn't mek no more baby.
Yes, me know bout hatred 'oman can have fi 'oman
fe nuh reason at all, an mi know say bad mine
sometimes worse dan obeah, an dat people can cubbitch yuh
fe nuttin at all, all fe yuh children dem,
even when yuh an dem a suffah, an a suck salt grain.

Dese same hands know how fe boil up castor oil fe speed up lazy baby
wash you in cerasee bath when you have chicken box
boil yuh tamarind tea when yuh have measles
wrap yuh fe sweat out good when you a roast wid dengue fever.

Dese hands is healing hands, hugging hands, and beating hands
to cut yuh lickle tail when yuh behave bad,
rub dixie peach and castor oil into your scalp
till yuh fall asleep, and a put yuh down beside me gentle.
Dese hands even teach yuh to pick rat-cut coffee beans, remember?

I woke up to a flood of memories long forgotten,
my pillow soaked in tears,
the mumps that I got the same day you died,
the long black hearse carrying your body past the gate
as I stood in what was left of the coffee walk —
the little bit the government had not killed with spraying.
Killing ganja, they said. Killing off de small coffee farmers, you said —
leaves, tied to my jaw to keep the swelling down,
held in place by a red kerchief,
the dull ache of the mumps competing with a tightness in my chest

my breathing shallow and labored
your loss weighting down my eight year old spirit,
as if I had been orphaned.

Mummah, I carried your picture home from England
and I know your spirit came with me
'cause I dream your plug tobacco,
smell the camphor, the pimento and the bay rum in your skin,
see you in the grandmothers waiting at the bus stop,
sitting in the pew across from me at church.

And often, when I forget the source of my own power,
it is your voice that soothes me still,
your hands rubbing bay rum into my neck,
that gets me through these nightmared days,
my dreams trailing red-ripe coffee beans,
leading from you and back to myself.

GRANDPA KNOLLIS

I can only harvest the pieces of you
from other people's memories
but I gather them anyway,
spread them out like a jigsaw puzzle
excitement mounting when pieces fit,
frustration multiplying when they don't.

I feel I must save your picture, cracked though it may be,
for the ones who will come after
and never hear your name, visit the old yard
or sweep the mango blossoms from your tomb.

Drop by drop memory collects like fresh rain water
leading from the corrugated zinc gutters on the roof
into the ancient oil drums at the back
of the house you built with my grandmother.
Watered by my incessant questions, the stories come to life:
the jacket and waistcoat you always wore
to Calpan Anglican church before it was blown down in '51 storm;
and the legend of you matching might with those formidable winds
bracing your 6ft 3, 250 pound bulk against the front door
through the long sleepless night, while the storm
demanded the sacrifice you refused to surrender
(taking parts of the zinc roof instead).

Your children remember the remnants of your Cuban past:
the smooth black stone that kept your water cool
in the bottom of the earthenware jar;
the wooden cane with the carved handle
you wore just so, across your right shoulder;
the trunk full of lace tablecloths,
thick bedspreads and heavy silver utensils
you brought from Havana for your bride –

and the frequent lapses into the rapid Spanish
my mother remembers as your language of anger.

Returning home after twenty years in exile
to marry the widow of a man with your surname.
a cousin perhaps, but with skin as near white
as yours was jet black
eyes flecked green where yours were a steady brown,
a man from a family so proud of their white ancestry
they never acknowledged my grandmother
until the children came red, light brown, puss-eyed?
You, with your own stubborn pride,
how could you stand being in a family that denied
the very source of your dashing good looks,
the powder-smooth black skin – always the first thing mentioned
after "he was a good looking man!"?

Another mystery to unravel –
digging under other people's refuse to unearth historic jewels –
was the Hispanic link in the naming of your children –
Miguel, Antonio, Isola –
mnemonic threads connecting to a boyhood,
and young manhood spent in Cuba?
When you joined your sister in the Panama Canal
it was not from Port Antonio or Kingston Harbour
as I had assumed, but from somewhere in Cuba,
whose name I may never learn
where you may have had a sweetheart, friends, children?

But the land you came home to, you left as my legacy,
my necessary, fractured past,
the land that nurtures my dreams
my need to struggle towards wholeness,
(in the face of the seductions of erasure
masquerading as cynicism and sophistication)
recognizing all the while that the struggle is the real prize ...

This land that you bought for your children,
and their children and their children's children
as a symbol of roots and permanence
could not, did not, nurture you to wholeness.
Whether in glorified hyperbole or watered down and tainted
all the stories paint you permanently displaced,
spiritually homeless, an outsider, unbelonging.

But you had the vision to foresee
that your children would need the grounding you never found.
Wide spaces of sky, fertile earth,
skin and kin they could lay claim to
and enough land to build houses and dreams...

So, I gather the fragments that left you outside history,
ordinary deeds and misdeeds — legendary temper, marital conflicts,
the whippings you gained village-wide fame for
(yes, the beatings still remembered
that makes it hard for some to speak of you)
and place them by my mother's stories of your tenderness to me,
gestures only my spirit remembers.

I must save them all,
pound them together into a bittersweet ball,
brown and oily like the chocolate
my grandmother used to make from scratch,
keep in a cupboard for when company calls,
generations of great and greater grandchildren
the newly exiled, homeless, permanently displaced.
From the pieces of this puzzle
imperfect, like the legacy you left us,
perhaps they will invent their own past
weave themselves a story with a middle,
a beginning, perhaps an end or two.

STORY FOR MAMA DAISY

It was a star-apple season in Woman Pond;
the crickets were rehearsing a symphony in the coffee walk.
Night had just fallen, sudden like the closing of the wooden shutter
and my uncles were gathered on the verandah
smoking Craven A's and telling ghost stories.
Uncle Wammy was telling the one about the rolling calf
that turned into a ball of fire and chased him all the way home,
when my father interrupted with a new story
about the duppy light that knocked down
the two church sisters coming home late from revival service.
You laughed so hard your waters broke,
and I slid down quick and slippery like a fish,
into my grandmother's waiting arms.
Hers was the first face I saw,
the woman we both called Mummah.

2

Seems you were always taking time away from telling me stories
to go off working somewhere, day's work at the Goldings
night shifts at the textile factory,
with periodic intervals of looking hard for work,
when you, too tired from worry, shuttered your face like night,
turned your stories off, and I went running
for refuge in Mummah's camphor-soaked bosom.

3

But I could have lived on your stories:
'Dame Round Face and the Magic Polisher';
or my favorite about Mummah saving the life
of that hateful woman who had a dead baby
stuck inside her. She hated my grandmother
for saving her life, but not the baby's. Stupid woman.

I could have lived on your stories,
but you insisted that I eat meat like other children,
wear pretty dresses, drink milk, and attend church
and school recitals, where I secretly pilfered
and performed your stories.

4

When I took to sitting in corners with books
you frowned, but said nothing.
What were you going to do with a child who ate books,
you who struggled to keep meat on the table?
And when Mummah died leaving you motherless,
and fully responsible for the children
she left you bereft and burdened.

5

So at 12 I left you for someone else's home,
someone who could afford to feed a child on books.
Our goodbye was two lonely backs turned
walking in opposite directions,
neither knowing if the other cried.
Restavec it is called in Haiti.
In Jamaica it is less common,
goes by no special name except survival,
but the terms of servitude are much the same,
the silences part of the game.

6

So I learned to love what could touch me without hurting,
what could disappear from my hands without leaving,
what could make me hunger, but never left me gasping for air:
I learned to love the books I ate,
because they taught me how to reproduce

the stories you had fed me with breast milk.
Now I do not know where you and I end
and the stories begin, and it doesn't matter any more.
Each time I find a new story, or a new way to tell an old one
I become a little more your daughter.

SPIRIT AND SOLE

1

These shoes, these shoes,
I hate these shoes,
big, black leather
clown shoes
one full size bigger than my feet
I won't polish and spit-shine them,
will break their backs down
on my way to school
climb to the top of the lime tree
jump down repeatedly

But one year of abuse
and they refused to spring a toe-hole
or burst out at the seams;
those shoes, my nemesis,
did not understand quit.
How could I get Mom to buy me
cheap pretty American shoes from Miami (via Haiti)
when you insisted on making my shoes indestructible?

2

I would come running to the gate
when I saw your car
not for the shoes
but to stare rudely at your children,
my rich cousins from town.

3

Watching you move across my grandmother's yard
was like watching a video in fast forward –
the jerking, quick-dragging walk up the rocky pathway
leading to our verandah, your curved, curlicued left foot
valiantly trying to keep up with the impatient tippy-toe
of your pointed right, the walk as much you as the shoe factory
in the back of your home in a good part of Kingston;
or the determined look that was your permanent mask,
an intense concentration punctuated occasionally
by a fast-breaking warm smile that lit your eyes;
or the way you spoke in short staccato sentences
delivering impartially greetings, news, or commands:
Double stitch the soles!
I must have been eleven or twelve before it occurred to me to ask,
"What happened to Uncle's foot?"
"Polio," someone said.
And then, "Im disable from pickney days."
Apparently, somebody forgot to tell you.

4

I write this now not to embarrass you
but to let you know your testament lives in me.
When life's handicaps seem insurmountable
I fast drag, haul ass, move
as if I was born with two perfect feet
and a factory in my own backyard
double stitching my soles, so even twisted,
curlicued and fractured, they move me onward.

OGUN

Uncle Miguel, slight of build, graying in his beard and hair,
never took a day off sick, so most days could be found
dipped in grease under the belly of a cheap Russian Lada.
He could take apart and put back together any car.
When I was fifteen, he built a Bedford truck from the axle up.
I was convinced it would never run, and lived to eat my words.

He took the engine, the clutch and gearbox
from Mass Tom's long defunct Leyland truck
that had spent its youth carrying market women from St. Catherine
to Parade, to sell long-stem Gross Mitchell bananas,
yellow-heart breadfruits, sugar-cane and sweet-jelly coconut.
The truck was living out its retirement under the mango tree
home for spiders and lizards, enjoying a second career
as a planter box for seedling mangoes, love-bush
and diverse wild plants, happily rusting away,
glad to be free of loud-talking market women
and idle, spliff-smoking side boys.

Other parts he hunted for in far-flung districts
and piece by piece put the truck together like a quilt.
If I close my eyes I still see the bright blue flames
dancing from the blow torch, melding metal to metal.
When it was almost finished it looked like a dog with mange,
with its multi-colored doors and pitch-patches everywhere,
but sanded, primed and painted a fresh bright red,
with yellow flames on the sides, it purred like the kitten
I wanted to take to school, to watch the envy of the kids with money,
as I staked my claim on what could be had without money.

But that was almost twenty years ago;
nowadays the village drivers bring him Camrys and Hondas.
He welcomes the change, the ease, but finds little challenge,
and even less earnings. Newer cars mean less work,

so he spends more time in the fields than he used to,
and these days is less opposed to travel and "foreign"
than when business was good.
Then he'd leave his house in the hills every morning
to come down to work at his 'garage',
my grandmother's yard, always full of cars, grease and laughter,
loud-talking men drowning-out my soft-spoken uncle
until you heard his low chuckle and trademark "Yes, man!"
Boys were initiated into manhood in the yard,
inhaling Craven A and guzzling warm Red Stripe beer
while they learned how to make a honest living,
and even how to "run a boat,"
making a fire under the jackfruit tree
and cooking white flour dumplings as big as wheels
with ackee and salt-fish swimming in coconut oil.

There was metal everywhere. I could even taste it
on the tongue of my first boyfriend,
feel it rubbing cold and comforting against my skin
as I savored my first Red Stripe beer-
dipped kiss under a sky so bright, so close
I could trace the milky way with my fingertips.
I still have scars on my legs
from bumping into car parts in the dark.
Even in the garden old axles and rims competed
with my mothers crotons and joseph coats.

Respected by men, loved or resented by women,
Uncle Miguel remains a man of contradictions.
He disliked short haircuts, but would never wear locks,
believing one 'don't haffi dread to be Rasta',
and earned the title "Jah Mig"
from that large following of boys he mentored,
boys he taught to drive and fix cars
giving them alternatives to farming,
(since teaching and preaching jobs were few and already taken),

men now, some in their forties, some scattered abroad
in New York, Ft. Lauderdale, Palm Beach, East London, L.A., Toronto –
or the few who remained in the village with him.

On my last visit to Jamaica,
I watched him cradle his granddaughter on his lap,
rocking her back and forth as he watched a cricket match on T.V.
and it came back to me how he'd raised four children alone
when his wife left, made sure they all got a good education
and went to church on the Sabbath, and still found time
to care for the children his sister left behind
for the greener pastures of New York.
And as I watched him rock,
rock, rock the little girl
who was drifting to sleep in his arms,
I was thinking,

"When I was a teenager, I used to think you were so serious,
so strict with me, you'd chase me home, tell me
to pick up a book if you caught me at a dance, scowl
when I got too chummy with a village boy...
But there's a tenderness in you that I've always felt,
a closeness I cannot put my finger on..."

He interrupted my thoughts,
as if he had been reading them,
and told me this story:

Just like dis, when you was a baby,
dis is how I used to put you to sleep.
Remember dat big rock dat used to be down by de gate?
Well, every evening, after dinner,
I used to take you from your madda,
and carry you down to the gate,
where mi and mi fren dem use to meet. Eh-eh,
all yuh fadda too. An ah use to rock yuh,

30

rock you, rock you, just like dis, till you drop off to sleep.
Jus like dis…"

So there it is, I thought as I stepped outside onto the verandah
breathed in the crisp night air and slowly exhaled,
clearing my eyes to make out the night garden of metal,
casting familiar shadows (but no longer competing
with my mother's crotons and joseph's coats) –
old cars stored beneath the mango tree
to be stripped of their useful parts,
unmarked taxi-cabs on cement blocks
awaiting a part from Kingston,
car parts looming like grotesque iron branches,
a garden of strange-shaped foliage
blooming like jasmines perfuming the clear St. Catherine night,
and the steady blue flames of the blowtorch
homage to Ogun,
smelting it all together.

OUTSIDE CHILE

Outside chile, yes! Born outta wedlock
one stormy October morning, 'cause her
Mammy say she too beautiful and proud
to marry the chile no-good, run-around, not-so-pretty daddy
although him did come from a bright family!

Well, this chile grow, have sense,
find her daddy well-married off
to a quiet, stay-at-home, wash-the-clothes, go-to-church
kind a woman. Nothing like she mammy.

Outside chile, she used to visit
at birthdays and Christmas time
to watch the crumbs falling off the plate
of the inside, bellyful children dem.

People used to ask,
Is dis de outside pickney?
Bway, but she almost pretty
look a little like her mammy
and a whole lot like her daddy-
side a people dem,
but de family don't accept her, nuh?

Big, bright-eyes, pretty, white smile
long, skinny legs, short, curly mop a reddish brown hair
(Mammy used to catch her and rub
black shoe-polish in her head,
nasty up de pickney white school-blouse)
smarter than a whip-lash
gentler than a Mama's tit
sensitive like a raw-nerve
exposed to cold and rain.

Big, nationwide exam
only ticket to high school fe all like she
likkle brown-dusk pickney
Passed with flying colors
name in all the papers, you know!

De whole village happy. Like Manley say,
No bastard no deh again, everyone lawful
and de bible say, *De stone dat de builder refuse*
will live fi tun head cornerstone.
But pickney don't business wid none a dat.
She jus want a lickle quiet time wid her mammy,
fe look up inna she flowers-pretty face,
ask her, *Did I make you proud?*

GROWING UP

Remembah when we did young
an' use to run up de hill fah watah?
Wi use to drink till wi belly favor
two roun' inflated balloon
an' run back dung de hill
listening to de chug-a-chug-a-lug
of watah mekkin' music inna we belly.

Mamma use to sey,
One a dese fine days, unnu belly gwine bus
wid all dat watah. Wha unnu drink su' much fah?

Now me running up de hill without yuh
an' some days de watah bittah.
Still mi jus cahn get ennuf
an' mamma no de yah fi warn me,
an' more time, me belly jus bus'

For my cousin Loris.

MANGO SEASON IN BOIS CONTENT

(for The Honorable Portia Simpson Miller
and the working class people of Jamaica)

Taking the roller-coaster ride round the winding green hills
where red dirt dyes the nimble feet of children
playing dandy-shandy on the St Catherine country roads,
I reached Bois Content, tranced in the midday heat,
a languor to fool the uninitiated
into thinking this village lived up to its name.

But as I drove along the roadside,
the image of ripe mangoes dancing like a one drop
in my head – Julie, Number 11, Common,
Blackie, Bombay, East Indian, Sweetie –
mangoes raining down like hailstones
mango fe stone dawg mi a tell yuh! –
I saw the trees were barren, naked of any fruit.

What happen to all the mangoes?
I asked my uncle, by way of greeting.
He shook his head and said:
Rain fall hard dis year and wash off all a de blossoms,
Water, water, water like dirt, me a tell yuh.
De whole place nearly wash way.
All some Rasta dung a Church Pen wash-out gaawn a sea,
Yuh nuh stay a foreign an hear?

Seeing my distress the village rallied round
with an offering of old fashioned goodness
country love so plentiful it shamed me,
every fruit in season, mine for the eating
till I was filled to bursting,
like the harvest festival at the Seventh Day Adventist Church

its arched pitch-pine doorway
decked with fresh green coconut fronds as if for a wedding,
its altar overflowing with jelly-coconuts, sweet sugarcane,
star-apples, pineapples, neaseberries, june plums,
sweet-sops, sour-sop, guava, ugli fruit, jackfruit,
stinking toe, passion fruit and more ...
Good, good nyamings to satisfy a half-life of yearning for home,
But... not one mango anywhere in Bois Content?

Still in disbelief, I went closer to inspect
the mango tree in Uncle Son's front yard,
expecting to see failure reflected in her branches.
But she did not look a bit defeated.
She looked fat and verdant,
her proud head spreading to the midday sun,
arms akimbo and bottom cockout like one sexy Jamaican woman's.

Then, hear what de mango tree say to me:

> *Me had a set back dis season*
> *but next year, watch me!*
> *Me a go shock out and grown nuff mango*
> *Me a go full every hungry belly a country*
> *and have nuff lef back fe sell a market*
> *yuh just watch me man, next year...*

Hear de mango tree, nuh?

> *You, me, Uncle Son, Miss Iris, Mass Tom, all a we*
> *we just a bide we time till next season*
> *We coming back live and direct, full force*
> *Yuh just watch we, next season*
> *we a go shock out*
> *We a go stand firm and put down roots too deep*
> *fe any lickle dibi-dibi hurricane fe come test we.*

De mango tree look pon me good and say,

> Cho! a true yuh no know we!
> We stronger dan all dis mess and botheration
> dis crime, corruption an' mass deportation
> dis spir-i-tual wic-ked-ness in high places!

De mango tree rock back, steady sheself and say,

> Mek me tell yuh someting,
> fe we faith can move Blue Mountain
> and full up Blue Hole.
> Jus watch we, man. We a go shock out!
> We a go show dem say a nuff sweet cassava grow we.

> Just wait and see, Next season!

'OMAN A SILK COTTON TREE

(for the women of Jamaica)

I am exposed, naked in
grandfather's studied indifference.

He walks through me with ease,
his one clear eye cuts me with such reckless abandon
I have to pinch my flesh to see if I am real.

I feel disembodied, transparent
my nostrils begin to burn
sweat breaks out on my upper lip,
on the bridge of my nose, as my anger rises.

But my rage feels impotent,
my legs grow numb
I try to lift them, but they will not budge.
I cannot feel my body and grow terrified.

My screams echo off the tops of high rises
tornado through whole cities,
laying them desolate.

I stand still in the ruins listening to the unearthly silence
wondering when my flesh will crumble and fall away,
as if I had never been…

Grandmother appears from the haze and smoke,
a mountain lion with softly padded claws.

Her clear bright eyes reflect sunset reds,
the mossy green of caves buried deep within the earth,
the purple of mountains I have not yet climbed,
and the warning streaks of a lightning storm

that will burn clean through street and bush,
to level everything.

She licks my skin and I am comforted,
my head nestles in her soft, downy bosom
she licks me raw with her roughened tongue
searing her words into my flesh.

I am permanently branded with her meanings
remembering all our desires and hurts,
our battered dreams,
our past and future journeys,
our blood-bought promises
our hopes for salvation,
redemption!

She implores me, none too gently:
Remember, mi daughter! Yuh haffi 'member dis.
Say it wid me now!

Banish and vanish a nuh de same ting;
spirit stronger dan flesh.
Nobaddy cyaan jus come wipe yuh out
unless ah yuh wan' dem to.
Spirit yuh can tief, but yuh cyaan kill.

Repeat after me, mi daughter:

'Oman is more dan flesh and blood
'Oman a silk cotton tree, inhabited by nuff live duppy
'Oman a sea-ball hole, yuh cyaan sight up de depths a she
'cause she run straight out to deep ocean water,
'Oman a rockstone a river bottom,
weh member every drop a water dat wash ovah she.

Yuh name 'oman. Nuh fraid a him.
Nuh fraid a none a dem.
Hold up yuh head and look pon him good!

See! A mad him mad!
An him a try fe mad yuh too,

Look!

See how him pants a drop offa him;
him a maager down.

Bide yuh time, mi pickney!

Fi we day just round de corner
Fe we day mus come!

LEAVING

"Who shall kindle the fire now
and pick the coffee at harvest time
feed the chickens
water the cows and goats
and boil green herbs
to bathe away
the baby's fever?"
"Not I", she said,
"surely,
not I,"
standing
half-in, half-out
the door,
the years falling naked
from her face!

For Mom, Curene and all the women who had the strength to walk away.

CRIOLLA: DE DIS/POSSESSED

A me dis – de bastard offspring
of de illicit affair, de outside chile
once remove from both sides.
Both a dem a try fe deny me
mi double birthright – dispossession!
No one nuh come fe claim I and I
so me climb up inna de cave
curl up with de snakes
and learn to whisper venom,
blow me snake-breath into de wind
embitter de firs' dust of spring pollen.
Bees come buzzing round me lap
creaming one love into me orifices;
me lend dem deceit fe sweeten dem sting.

Me is de outside chile, de illegitimate one.
Mother toss back her head, declare herself unwilling,
unwitting accomplice in mi conception,
declare me bastard, corrupt like me daddy passion,
birthed me at de mouth of de cavern
and return to Prospero
unblemish from her nights of sin.

Me know seh a lie she deh tell.
See her deh look back wistful,
but unlike Lot's wife me Madda tears nuh turn her to salt
but render her more pliant, more credible.
Who not gwine believe de tale she tell
wid her lip dem a tremble
and her eye dem swell up from one piece a bawlin'.

Me deh yah de suck snake venom
while she squeeze out de milk she have fi me
from outta her breasts pon de fire-hearth stone dem.

Hear de tortured sizzle as she drain herself dry
(and dem claim dem never learn nuttin from mi granny)
while me de dead fe hungry, ban mi belly,
swallow bile with de venom and grow forked tongue
dat stretch the length of fern gully,
grow verdant and supple like alan bamboo
reaching round worlds and back to this little piece of rock
where me stretch out, shed me skin like croakin' lizard
and wait for de day when me nuh longer wait...

Fadda nuh dare look pon me.
Him talk to mi wid im back turn,
name de worlds I and I see
and de faces that refuse to see me.
Me learn de rhythm of him voice,
each curve and dip, swell and whirl,
syllable by syllable me swallow him meaning whole
until me learn to speak in parables like de river.

Now dem bound to hear, though dem still don't see me,
misnaming me Cali or Mira when me is neither,
just me in multiplicity, me oneness, me own
although me nuh have nuh face.
Yet me will roar yuh thunderous ululations,
mock yuh safety, yuh sureness of self,
till I and I become de bo in bombo, eloquent and sacrilegious.
Yuh will love me yet, know me, name me right
when me upset de table at yuh dinner-party,
turn over de dutchie pot off de pimento wood fire,
dumpling turn to ashes, caviar nestling in vomit.

Say yeah, a me rule
fire an' brimstone to rass!
A weh oonuu tek dis ting fah?

CONFESSIONS OF A RESTAVEC

1

Floating in a clear shallow river
fragrant with oranges
holding two black shiny bubby biters
to each small honey-coated breast
river stones graze my back,
as I pray for fullness.
I am dreaming of my mother,
pretty as a daisy
whose face I don't deserve to see.

2

There is someone watching over me,
but today she's way up past the clouds.
There *is* someone standing by the hog pen,
watching me. I hope it's my classmate Carlos,
but I know it's his older brother Franky.

3

No one touches me here,
but hot words sear my flesh wide open
rubbing pepper into wet places that never heal.
Things fester here,
but nothing is allowed to die.

4

There is a library full of books
for me to feed on,
to ward off loneliness, evil.

5

Lord of hosts, the gods are angry with me.
I have washed in the sweet lamb's blood
to get to your throne of grace,
pushed past the mysteries of your distant,
vast incomprehensibility,
alienating gods and lesser mediums
in my ascent.
Do not forsake me now.

EXILED MUSINGS

HALLELUJAH IN THE MIDDLE

Hell a top, hell a bottom
hallelujah in the middle
Come on, Granny,
don't fade away on me now
I need the rest of this recipe.

Say is not recipe is riddle.
Well, Gran, riddle or recipe
is all de same to me...
Please Gran, wid all due respec', ma'am
I don't want to hear dat yuh dead and gone,
yuh see de size a dis pumpkin belly?
What I s'pose to tell dis chile?
Dat I don't know wat to put on scorpion bite
'cause yuh dead and gone?

Awright, awright, mi Granny,
don't get cross
don't bother bite-off me head!
'cause I ain' finish wid you yet
and anyway, ef yuh did tell me long time
I wouldn't have to come ask you for it now.

I need to know where to bury de navel string
how much leaf of life to put in de bush bath
how fe time de sweet potato pudding
so it come out custard sof pon top.

Granny, tell me again, ma'am,
jus how much hell me have fe build up pon de top
fe balance de fire glowing red hot down a bottom!
And how fe temper de heat from rising up too fast
so me don't tek careless and burn up all a me sweetness!

An' jus' one more ting, please, Gran,
before yuh go back when yuh come from,
teach me how fe hold on
to de hallelujah in de middle!

MIGRATORY PATTERNS

It's natural for birds to fly south in winter
but we fly north in every season
leaving warmth in search of dreams
that sometimes leave us cold.

Like birds of a feather we fly in formation,
vulnerable at hunting season
yet do not stop or break our ranks
when one of us falls victim
to the hunters' need for feathery trophies.

You will find us in Flatbush, Brixton, Toronto, Queens,
huddled against the cold in the New York winter,
sweating in the merciless Miami summer,
waiting at the bus-stop, the tube station, the subway,
catching the #4 Bus to the E train to Queens Blvd,
working for the same agency for thirty odd years,
taking care of the elderly sick
(till we ourselves become elderly and sick),
receiving promises for our years of service,
but constantly pushed aside for younger,
newer immigrants who can be paid the minimum wage.

Now we are placed "on call" which means...
after thirty odd years of putting up with
sexual abuse from the male patients,
and racial insults from people in general,
we are cut back to 24 hour weekend jobs which means...
keeping watch over patients at night which sometimes means...
being forbidden to heat our food or store it in their fridge
which means...
eating cold or stale food for two nights, which means ...
being accused of neglecting or abusing patients
if we fall asleep and they fall out of bed, which means...

being glad to return to our comfortable homes in St. Albans,
to the houses we bought making $7.50 an hour
in the good old days when work was plenty
and the 1199 union was strong.

Yet, you will still find us buying houses in St. Albans,
Coral Springs, Sheffield and Birmingham,
brightening classrooms at Harvard, Rutgers and Berkeley,
running for political office, owning grocery stores
and restaurants, striving and surviving
against all odds, defying all statistics,
moving in formation and never looking back
when some of us fall prey to the hunt
and descend, wings clipped, in a downward spiral.

Awaiting deportation in INS jails
the disillusioned offspring of those made redundant,
after thirty years in the same menial jobs,
watch their parent's limp-winged descent
and grow hard and cold watching music videos
and box-office movies showing who is really living large
and who benefits from whose hard work.
The lesson they learn is that it is better
to be a hunter than a migratory bird.

It is natural for birds to fly south in winter,
but Caribbean people fly north in every season
leaving the warmth of familiarity and family
in search of dreams that sometimes leave us freezing in the snow.

DIS MAN'S COUNTRY

What if we were to tell the truth
about the immigrant experience
the Caribbean immigrant experience,
the Black Caribbean immigrant experience?
Would we tell of the bitterness of defeat
when our dreams did not materialize
exactly the way we planned them?

How we fretted when that job did not come through,
or when the business into which we'd dumped our savings
was not such a great success, but we kept it going anyway,
year after bloody year, because we'd left our little piece of rock,
come to this man's country to make a life
and failure was not an option.

What if we were to tell the truth about our voluntary exile?
That we became the butt of jokes *In Living Color*
for the three, four jobs we worked
to make down-payment on that modest home,
since owning a home expressed the dogged determination
that cast our spirits in iron, made us oblivious
to racial slights and other insults
we broaden our backs to take daily.

What if we were to tell the relatives we support back home,
the ones who believe we pick up money off the streets,
the ones who call us all kinds of mean and stingy
when we do not send the dollars they ask for,
the computer they need, the designer shoes they must have,
what if we were to tell them some of us do not have
designer shoes, computers, or dollars to spare,
because after we've paid Uncle Sam,
Auntie Visa, Cousin Rent or Grandpa Mortgage,
Mumma Hungry Belly and Pickney School Shoes

demanded what was left, and many days we were as broke
as they back home, but in much more debt?

What does it mean to be a model minority one month
and a sniper suspects the next?
How does it feel to have our image tarnished
by intermittent violence, civil unrest,
persistent poverty and political corruption in our island homes?
To risk our lives in makeshift boats
then suffer the indignity of being
locked down in Krome detention center
because we are not from the right piece of rock
and our suffering does not serve a political agenda,
and the tragic faces of *our* dark babies
do not make American mothers weep
or write their congressman?

Who keeps the statistics on high blood pressure in our community,
or the rates of diabetes, HIV, heart attacks, cancer and strokes?
Depression, schizophrenia? How are we doing with these?
How many of us suffer from poor eating habits,
poor living habits, poor praying habits…?

If we were to tell the truth sometimes,
we would have to admit that life in dis man's country
is not everything it's cracked up to be.
So what is the source of our strength?
How do we survive the racism and despair,
when the system cheats us of our right to vote
and challenges the way we raise our children,
when we become targets of police brutality,
unfairly subjected to deportation?
How do we continue to claw our way up, sometimes on bloody knees,
making millions for Uncle Sam and Sir Western Union
while our hard-earned dollars shore up the economies
of our small island nations?

If we were to always tell the truth
we would say we survive by faith and only by faith,
no matter what name we call in prayer.
An exiled people, orphaned from our homes,
alienated sometimes from our very roots,
God's goodness we never question,
for instinctively our spirits know
never to stray too far from the source of all strength,
because, despite advancements of every kind,
God's grace is still the most amazing!

DEAD LEF DUTTY TUFF

Me sey, di ole people dem dead lef lan
is a caution an' a comfort when yuh de a foreign.
Wedder yuh de box bread outta hog mout
or you de live large abroad, yuh glad fe know sey it de deh,
jus in case yuh haffi run back a yuh yard
wid one shut pan yuh back,
even if di house full up a generation
an yuh haffi pitch tent so gwaan rough it,
nobaddy cyaan run yuh off a de dead lef lan
weh yuh dead granddi dem lef fe all a oonu.
It de deh dah wait pon yuh fe wen trouble tek yuh
and pickney shut de fit yuh.

Me sey, all dem smaddy weh use fe cuss country
and tek wi thatch-roof house, and we drum-pan water
so throw inna we face,
gwine glad fe some so-so breadfruit
wid rundung, hours beat…

Missis, inna dem yah time,
when Bin Ladin bin a mek Merka go up gum tree,
when fire de a mus-mus tail
an im de fret sey di cool breeze
im tink im feel might be something else,
something fi wipe im offa di slate,
it good fe know sey we ole people dem
did tug-u-tug-u and wuk from cyaan-see to cyaan-see,
and pull cassava, and reap coffee and pimento,
and raise trenton, and pad up donkey go a market before day bruk,
from Thursday thru Sattiday every week,
and even tek boat go a Panama fe wuk inna de muck,
and get denge fever and chigga,
an dead or nearly dead fe build backra canal,
fe mek smaddy else prosper.

But de ole timers dem, dem never complain,
dem is wha yuh call real Jamaicans,
dem nuh fraid a hard wuk, dem nuh mek excuse,
so long as dem back strong and dem caan get outta de bed
all wen dem caan hardly manage, dem jus a grunt an tek it,
dem add up every lickle mickle mek a muckle
throw dem one one coco inna de basket
till dem save enough fe come back a yard
come buy piece a dutty tuff, way up past God back
(cause who can afford low land?).
It far up inna bush, an it nuh mek it pan di map
so nuh touris' cyaan find it (which is alright wid some a wi)
but it pretty an green, an di hill top view nice,
nuff water de a river, and yuh caan still catch crawfish fe yuh dinner,
de mango dem sweet and plenty,
an de yellow heart breadfruit dem big, and eat better than bread
(though when saltfish scarce or money nuh nuff,
yuh haffi eat dem wid so-so ackee).

Di dirt red and stain yuh foot bottom
and if yuh doan' wear shoes, yuh foot bound fe crack,
but is family land, so whether yuh hate it or yuh love it,
it cyaan sell, but must tan deh fe de pickney dem
Even de facety Mercan one dem, who no business wid it
still it did deh fe dem, and fi wi, jus in case trouble tek wi
an wi haffi find wi roost like fowl.
It good fe know sey, di dead lef lan de a yard,
de piece a dutty tuf, weh Grandi dem wuk out dem soul-case fah,
nuh gaan no weh, it still de a country, up inna de bush
Yeh man, it de deh,
Di dead lef lan, still de deh!

CLIMBING

We clamber up
some fast, some slow
each striving to reach
the next level up
forgetting roots
our truths,

forgetting to stop and pick up
those who have fallen,
disgraced.
Disgrace.   Pshaw!

Disconnect and move
Cut and keep going
Clear and move
Move and move and move
And keep on moving upwards
Cut the sluggish ones off,
Pshaw! Dem too slow,
Holding us back.

We must
We must
We must
Keep moving
Till we forget where we
are coming from.
Till we forget
what we are running from.

SNAPSHOTS, HEADLINES AND CLIPPINGS

In West African philosophy, time is measured not by
a linear movement of hands across the face of a clock
but by the events that occur in our daily lives,
so when the phone rings at 4 in the morning
and i croak, "Ma, is 4 a.m."
She says, "But dere's an earthquake in LA."
"But ah live in Berkeley, and ah tired," i say;
she sucks her teeth and says:
"Missis, git up out de bed and tun on the T.V."

And like the good Jamaican girl i was raised to be,
but often am not, i obey my mother,
'cuz see, i got used to 4 a.m. phone calls
way before i knew the heavy-eyed,
shuffling response to my son's call for four a.m. feedings,
like any working-class woman-of-color
who has brothers, fathers, sons, cousins
in any inner-city, anywhere in this beautiful mosaic of madness,
this melting pot of black-eyed peas and lynch-ropes,
fried plantains and burning crosses,
blood-puddings and blood-baths....

i am familiar with the fetid smell of fear;
it invades our bodies, seeps out of our pores
congeals the blood when the phone finally rings
after hours of waiting for that one phone call, allowed only
when the arresting officer is good and ready.

Tethered on the edge of manhood
our young men are afraid to make that final leap
lest, like Amadou Diallo, their gesture be mistaken
as reaching for that imaginary gun they're carrying.
So we watch with a mixture of dread and pride
as they lock their hair into beautiful coils of Afrocentric pride,

knowing it is yet another marker of difference
that will label them radical = dangerous = criminal
= targets

And yes, it is hard and insulting and necessary
to look at your brother-nephew-son
from the perspective of the woman who clutches her handbag
as he bops by her — head down
completely unaware of her existence,
for you still remember making up games
to get him to brush his teeth,
watching him fly, barefoot, through loose red dirt,
bucking his toe and coming running,
snot dripping down his nose,
for that magic sister-auntie-mother spit
that's gonna make it all better
and — like a mother who has too many children,
and a fading memory — i still go through all my brother's names
when i'm trying to summon my son
So we do not/cannot turn the phone off
so sure that one of these days
the inevitable is going to happen
while we're sleeping, making love, writing poetry
or just too damn busy to answer the phone.

i still wake for my son's 4'o'clock feeding
anticipating the day he will be too macho to say
"I want Mami, I got a oouie..."
for i have no cure for the disease
that will transform him from cute to criminal
in the gaze of a racist world
that both needs and creates these categories
for its own survival.

So when my neighbor watches nervously
as her daughter and my son play together,

her anxiety makes me jittery.
i ask, "Well, what is it, are they playing or fighting?"
She says, "They're playing, but I'm afraid it will escalate."

E S C A L A T E

the word hangs in the air, like a noose waiting for a neck.
Escalate into what? i want to ask, to say something acerbic like,
"Well, i removed the oozie from his diaper just this morning,"
but i say nothing, for the sound of her meaning,
stripped naked of its pretences and shoved back at her,
would somehow find a way to ricochet back on me,
the crazy black bitch she always knew i was
so i say nothing,
just let the word hang there like a death sentence

ESCALATE

creates its own images
develops its own myths of origin
tells its own sordid tale

ESCALATE

> Confrontation between the Inkatha Freedom Party
> and the ANC escalated into violence in the province
> of Natal, South Africa today, 300 ANC supporters
> were massacred

A ghastly patchwork quilt of dead Black bodies adorns the 6 o'clock,
painted zulus wearing traditional war-gear
dance across the screen, balancing spears on their shoulders
three days later Buthelezi shakes hands with de Klerk
and Mandela for international television.
Instead of his war-gear Buthelezi wears a suit
and a smile that doesn't quite reach his eyes.

ESCALATE

> Gang violence escalates in South Central LA claim-
> ing yet another young life... Black on Black Vio-
> lence has escalated to enormous proportions in New
> York City in the past decade...

The gaze never focuses on the root of any of these problems.
Zulus are scapegoats for violence in the townships,
and if you can keep the Negroes killing each other
they won't have time to fight their oppressors,
and not one drop of white blood will be spilled
in South Africa or South Central,
while the world waits expectantly for another *democratic election*
for as history teaches us over and over again
when the smoke clears up
there will be fewer Black people left
to fight over a tiny piece of mock apple pie
and Blacks in South Africa
will be about as free as Blacks in South Central, Brooklyn, Detroit,
Opa Locka, Oakland, Tivoli Gardens, Hollis, Flatbush, Brixton,
South London, Birmingham...
and the new blood yet to be spilled will travel
in a dark red stream down into the very center of the earth
to fuel the fire at the earth's core!

So do not wonder at the frequency of earthquakes, fires and floods
or the novelty of two year old Black boys learning to say Malcolm,
or even pretend to wonder at the righteous anger of Black mothers,
for even when you force us to bite our tongues into tiny fragments
we will still harness the strength of Harriet,
the boldness of Malcolm
the honesty of Audre
the brilliance of Zora
the genius of Rodney
the love of Barbara
the sweetness of Langston

the courage of June
the vision of Bob
the magic of Nanny
the pride of Garvey
the revolutionary spirit of Toussaint
the faith of my grandmother Matilda,
and the undefeated hope of all those nameless,
faceless Africans who worked and endured
fought and died
struggled and overcame
so we could survive…

Together,
we will spit the bloody pieces of our severed tongues into your faces,
grow new tongues in places that will surprise you.
From the roots of the old tree, newer and stronger trees will spring up.
Let all who believe in the power of the people say,
Ashe!

A SISTAH NEEDS LOVE *AND OTHER WEAPONS...*

Rage has tied my tongue
spun a web of silence round my pen.
I walk this cold night naked, unarmed, searching
for my lost words, trying to resurrect
the active-anger spilling from my pen
for Eleanor Bumpers, Michael Griffith,
but for you, my brother,
I can find no words,
locked up in the image of your cage,
long skinny hands handcuffed behind your back,
your seventeen-year-old righteous defiance
demanding to know *Since when*
was it a crime to play REGGAE
music from a boom box at the bus-stop?
I sit in the court house screaming
silent curses at the cold white
rightness, Soweto seeping into Queens, New York,
my brother another innocent victim.

2

He used to tell me I was just being prejudiced
when I warned BEWARE of white cops
white laws, white lies.
Last night I called to assure him
that I would cut my class to be there.
He said he knew!

He said every time now
he sees a white face in the neighborhood
terror rises in his throat
threatening to choke

I remind him of the time
I was five and he was one
and it was election season in Jamaica
There were the usual riots in the streets
someone threw tear gas
and I panicked!

I didn't know what to do with that
beautiful, brown-skinned
roly-poly, real live dolly-baby
Mama had left in my care,
so I laid him on the ground
and laid my body across his
I revived moments later to find him
screaming like a siren in my ear.

But that was when he was one,
small enough to hide beneath my body.
At seventeen he's six feet tall
and black and male and threatening
and the hungry white wolves
are howling for his blood
and sistah love is not big enough
sistah love is not deep enough
sistah love is not enough-enough
to protect him!

RELATIVITY

The red green hills of St. Catherine
don't mean shit in a two-storey
cold-water walk-up
a tight, mean hallway
where the zipped red face
of the neighbor is a heavy door
slammed shut,

and the only safe exit
is through the fire escape
to wash your Easter
bun and cheese down
with a Colt 45
(in a brown paper bag).

But it is Good Friday.
and Ma is clocking a 24/7 live-in shift
so you still observe
a meatless tradition –
although you have to do without
the fried fish and bammy
though, thankfully, no Easter Sunday
button-downs and vaselined legs.

This tar beach strewn with
empty 40s and burnt down blunt tips
amidst Ma's wilting potted creepers
definitely ain't no Faith Ringgold painting!

PUNKED

So let me get dis straight.
What were you tinking?

You were tinking that yuh boys
woulda tink yuh a punk
if yuh run fe yuh life.
So yuh did what?

Oh. Yuh were tinking
dat since de bullets missed yuh head
pierced your car windshield and went clean
thru to lodge in the back leather seat
'stead of blowing a hole clear
thru yuh head,
yuh had a duty to yuh boys
to return to the scene
gun pon cock,
dutty harry style
to lay claim to yuh challenged manhood?

Alright. I tink I understand.
Yuh were jus tinking of yuh boys.
Protecting yuh rep.
Well, weh yuh boys dem deh now
as yuh sit in dis cell
doing the time fe de crime?
Dat is not self defense
wen yuh tun vigilante.
Me no see no sign ah yuh boys!

Me see yuh wall line wid pictures:
yuh mama, yuh sister,
yuh datah and baby madda
yuh fadda and all yuh bredda dem

but me no see no picture of yuh bredren dem,
yuh boys!

Do, no say me fast,
but me nuh see yuh bredren dem come fe visit.
Is only yuh madda me see
come here once a month
An last time yuh sistah come
dem mek she tek off her brassiere
say de metal hook set off de monitor.
Is only dem me see a hug yuh up tight
and a cry every time dem haffi lef yuh.
Is dem a suffer, an a do de time wid yuh.
Yuh bredren dem nuh write, dem no come,
yuh sure dem is yuh boys?

But wat a nice lickle girl, yuh datah.
Yuh never did a tink bout she?
Is who gwine mine her now yuh gaan?
And yuh baby-madda stop come long time;
yuh caan blame her if she find another man
And yuh madda, one sweet lady,
she look so tired when she get off de bus
An she always burden wid package
food and what-not fe yuh
Yuh mind never did run pon she?

No? Oh, I understand.
Yuh were tinking of yuh boys,
yuh breddren, and yuh rep.
From a certain cock-eye angle,
it mek sense. But for 5-10? Is a pity....

THE UNSPEAKABLE

i'll be alright for days
weeks
a month
or two
look at the picture of you
holding my son
smiling
i smile back
easy
reassured
your spirit is unchained

then one day
i'll go by a mirror
see your eyes
looking back out of my face
pleading
or sitting down to dinner
see the profile of your head
in the way my son's lock
falls the wrong way
onto his plate
i reach over to right it
feel the unsummoned wet
like drowning,
splashing into his rice and peas
watering down my best sorrel

Then heart's sudden twist
anguished
open-mouthed
soundless scream
so loud inside
my head

it momentarily
deafens me
jaws ache from ear to ear
from trying not to scream
never knew it could hurt physically
this missing you,
my brother, my heart.

ON THE DOWN LOW

Up in here you either do the time
or let the time do you.
Some brothers get religion
some brothers sell their souls
some brothers sell themselves any line
like these down low brothers
lining up for Shaqueen
telling themselves if you only give,
you are not a queer,
or worse still,
you cannot get the deadly Hi Five
if you never receive.

Up in here,
brothers on the D.L.
if they make it out alive
still be on the down low
spreading the deadly Hi 5
to unsuspecting sistahs
Won't somebody
take that to the CDC
or whoever gives a damn!

SALSA REGGAE JAZZ BLUES

Moon rides high on 125th on Lennox
Hot Harlem nights
I'm ready for the ride
Beautiful blue-black Senegalese men
all dressed in white
peddle kinaras and cowery-shell necklaces.
I never see their women.

Sinbad rides a white Benz
into the Apollo
I stay outside to watch the fly girls
in tight mini-dresses and page-boy weave-ons
line up for a ticket
content myself with peppermint soap
and scented candles
from 125th Street Mart
Tomorrow is another day
got the rent to pay.

Catch the #2 train and pray
I make it to a seat on time
Catch the #2 train and pray
I get a car with a guardian angel
Catch the #2 train and pray
I make it home alive.

Hot wired, crack vials, gunshots pop
many blocks away
its the movies Jack/don't crack
New Jack City got a monkey on its back.

Look at me class
I'm a bird, I'm a plane, I'm the myth
of the Black Superwoman
I teach teenage mothers and wanna-be drug lords
Audre Lorde and Sonia Sanchez
Langston Hughes and Malcolm X
They write me love poems
send me hate mail
say I can't walk the streets again
I let it slide/I don't hide
Jungle love is tough Jack
survival of the luckiest.

Say, what's a nice middle-class boy like you
doing in my neighborhood?
Wanna go for a splash under the fire hydrant?
Black, brown, yellow-skinned
kinky, curly, nappy-headed children flip
take a dip, cool down
under the side-walk waterfall
This is our Jones beach/deal Jack
Queen of hearts or ace of spades
don't crack, its only love
on a hot Harlem night.

Salsa and Reggae coming through my window
Come on baby, let's do the cha-cha
rub-a-dub, rub-a-dub, rub-a-dub, a-dub-dub
lambada love,
and my black skin 'gainst your brown skin,
pretty as a picture
"I don't wanna wait in vain for your love"
'cause, "cold ground was my bed last night
and rockstone was my pillow,
ooh, oooh, oooh, oooh"

ACCIDENTALLY ON PURPOSE

So much easier to call this fullness accident
lest folks think you lack ambition,
commonsense, feminist ideals,
though everyone knows
to stumble unprotected
into passion these days
is courting either life or death,
sometimes both.

So we pretend we didn't imagine
how her hair would curl
her little fingers clench
or the smile play upon her lips
as she sleeps

We pretend we didn't wonder
whose temper he'd inherit
if he'd prefer peas to carrots
or whether he'd wake up crying at midnight
or sleep through an earthquake

We pretend we didn't close our minds
to the dreadful possibility
of poems left unwritten
dissertations half-done
or parties unattended

We pretend it never crossed our minds
all the conferences and lectures we'd miss
while playing peek-a-boo in the mirror
bringing down a fever
or taking a walk to the kiddy park
to play in the sand-box

We pretended surprise
when the lab report came back positive
Then we went home to consider the options
and after much thoughtful deliberation
decided against an abortion
Then, we spent loving hours
studying the pages of the name books
and when friends and concerned colleagues ask
we name the growing fullness .... accident.

CHENJERAI

What's in a name they will say,
difficult, exotic, different.
My son, I want you to tell them
Chenjerai means brilliant
stars lighting the stairs to the pyramids
Chenjerai means clever
B'rer Anansi outsmarting Bre'r Fox.

Chenjerai means genius, the Dogon
discovering astrology and astronomy
the Egyptians inventing Mathematics
Harriet Tubman birthing freedom
on the underground railroad
Nanny leading her troops to victory
against the British soldiers
Grandma Matilda reaching greased hands
into a swollen belly, extracting death
so that the living may live.
Hoary-headed ancestors storing history
like water in a calabash
passing down life-giving truth
from generation to generation.

Chenjerai, I want you to tell them,
tell yourself, you are more than nameless,
faceless, invisible soon to be obsolete black man/child
lurking in the back alleys of Amerika's mind
Chenjerai is a name much loved
among the Shona people of Zimbabwe
they believe every child should have
a name that means something,
a name to live up to.

So when they ask why your mother
named you Chenjerai,
tell them your mother is a poet, griot,
keeper of the secrets of your people
She knew you would face ignorance, even amnesia
about the contribution of our people
in this land that is not your home
and named you a promise of greatness,
and a hope of better things to come.
Let all who believe in the power of love
say, Ashe.

LOVE IYAH

My defiant child,
with the flying red locks
dread locks
framing a bright round face
so sharp,
so sharp
adult conversations must be coded,
triple coded
so nothing leaks out
to leap back and bite!

Quick to make friends
equally adept at flying-fisted rage
tears so close,
so close
they brim over
like an overfilled water-drum
even when you win.

Watching you race down the block
outstripping older boys
I pray silently,
loudly,
earnestly,
I pray
for strong, calm winds
to guide those winged feet
I love,
Iyah!

AN ON-GOING CONVERSATION

Daily we must fight
for the same crumbs
knowing neither rest nor respite,
breaking the same stones
to build the same road
to journey on without end,
lugging the same old loads
avoiding the same cracks
(that broke our mothers' backs).

And yes…
even in sleep
we must keep
that third eye open
listen for the approach
of the white-bellied rat
that blows first
to numb the spot
before it bites

bites and blows
bites and blows

numbing us further into sleep…
till we awake to bleeding heels
a gnawed-off knuckle
a frayed spine
that cannot support
our own familiar weight.

We must keep a steady vigil
have our grigris prepared
to ward off creeping evil

We must grow ears
in the soles of our feet
(the better to hear the earth's counsel)
eyes in the back of our throats
so we do not swallow
poisoned words
from smiling, well-meaning lips.

Sometimes we have to lie still
in a dark, quiet place
and listen to our inside voices
and the voices of our ancestors
warning us of danger,
teaching us how to proceed,
reminding us that though
we will emerge battle-scarred and tired,
and often sick and tired of always
being sick and tired,
we cannot, must not give in,
or only pass the baton when we have to,
must claim the right to defend the selves
we fight daily to preserve.

For Barbara Christian, with love and nuff positive light.

SOUTH FLORIDA SHOWER

(For my sister, Heather Andrade)

Have you ever been surprised
by a South Florida shower
the door of heaven opening abruptly,
dumping bucketfuls onto your unsuspecting head?
God, a mischievous child romping
your life into divine order,
legs flying every which way
you run pell-mell through the overfilled parking lot,
(forgetting dignity)
thru foggy lenses you fumble for the keys
to your oversized, overpriced SUV,
breathless, you reach the door of your car
yank it open, drop heavily into your seat
laughing, breath coming in ragged gasps,
sticking your tongue out to lick the raindrops
from your lips & taste the lingering sweetness
from the forbidden bear claw you had for lunch
(eaten on the run, at your desk)
mingling with the saltiness of sudden sweat
and something else you can't remember eating…

Musing on the inevitable rain-induced pile-up on I95,
(inept multi-taskers turned cell-phone junkies
swerving into calamity after near calamity)
the obligatory five police cars and two ambulances
at the scene of one fender bender,
and the indefatigable rubber-neckers
slowing traffic down to a grinding halt,
you sit in the warm, calm safety of the unmoving vehicle,
catching your breath, reluctant to join the melee
content to sit for a little while and watch
the fat raindrops rolling down fast
and hard like teardrops on the windscreen

the palm trees shivering in ecstasy,
dark and wet with delight
the whole world slick, drenched happy
in the innocence of midday.

HEART WARS

ELEGUA

Drape me in midnight blue-black and crimson
Color me blood-red hibiscus and nightshade
in the bewitching hour of our special day
Light a candle to bless our union
Share some Blue Mountain coffee
(with condensed milk for me)
and a nice Cuban cigar,
hmmnn, this is not a bad beginning ...

Drape me in silks and beads
anoint my shoulders with olive oil
quench my thirst with 100% over-proof
Jamaican rum and coconut water
Unwind me, consume me,
stretch me supple in your heated embrace.

Unhinge me in the glow of your midday sun,
blind me to the physical,
so my eyes turn inward to see the glow
of our double-fire
Help me feed this need,
a love divine,
a sacrifice so fine,
thick and rich and golden like palm oil.

Unravel my many mysteries
know me like the cowrie knows the ocean floor
Scrape me clean of debris so my amber will shine,
uncover me, reveal my dark mystique
to the uninitiated ones
Show them the power of a love divine,
that defies understanding
a love profound that hides nothing.

Steer me from the edge of the precipice,
snatch me from the arms of the mountain lion,
rescue me from twice-told lies
and the skin-teeth that is not a smile.

Help me feed this need
and find my deliverance
in the fullness of time.

MISUNDERSTANDING

(or Feminism is really very simple!)

When I said I did not want you
to shower me with roses
pay for my drinks
wine me and dine me
and grind me on the dance floor,
if doing all that
meant that you'd have the right
to command me
Lie down!
Get up!
Open up!
Shut up!
at your whim and whimsy,
I didn't mean
that you should send me
a basket of dead roses for a valentine
borrow my rent money,
leave empty milk cartons in my refrigerator,
and I certainly did not mean
that you should turn
my side of the bed
into the Arctic circle,
me a floating glacier
freezing in my own
cold zone,
I only meant
that you should… do me, baby
like you would have me… do you,
or someone else will be doing
the things you looove
to do!

JIGSAW NOOSE

1

I know a man whose words
form a jigsaw puzzle
in his brain
jump from his mouth
in a superfluous jumble
and lie listless
on the startled air.
His Mama boasts him brilliant
'cause she no longer understands
a word he says.

2

I know a man
who sculpted words,
molded them soft and round
like lullabies
to settle gently
round women's necks
like a widow's shawl
or a hangman's noose!

3

I know a man
whose chiseled words
shoot from his mouth
red hot with razor-
sharp edges
to lodge in the brain
to lodge in the brain like
a splinter of truth!

WRONG OR RIGHT, I CHOOSE...

And should I have stood there quietly
in that dark corner waiting
for you to ask me for a dance?
Should I have waited and for how long?
Would you have noticed my quiet confidence,
read the ancient beauty in the turn of my head,
the proud tilt of my chin?

I am velvety black and beautiful like the night
like the black magical women of legend,
I can blend in or stand out as I deem necessary,
yet I often go unnoticed by black men
whose eyes have grown accustomed
to reading beauty in gyrating female bodies
on music videos.

So, I chose you.
man, fed on my grandmother's rundown
and roast breadfruit, ackee and white yam.
I chose you,
man of my St. Catherine moonshine nights,
of ring games and Anansi stories
and patois speaking children
catching peeni-wallies in a bottle.

And now, here I stand
naked and whole
on a cracked Harlem Street
naked, so you can see
there are no razors in my bra
nor explosives under my skirt
I have no other motive
but love,
though I chose you.

A TRINIDADIAN SANKE
(for my rebel youth)

This child is an acrobat
doing flip flops
somersaulting 'gainst me ribs
This child is a saga bway
yelling bacchanal,
look now is carnival!
at 2 a.m. in the morning

This boy is a drumming boy
pounding out messages
to the villages inside me womb
This child is a badjohn
will stick fight with anyone,
winding and grinding with the band
This child is no mistake
he just come to test me faith
Listen, Shango breaking thunder
at his birth.

RONKE TELLS ME

Ronke tells me
when you love a man
you want to make an image
of him and you as one
and I laugh,
for this goes against everything I believe,
in theory.

Yet, I search my mind
and cannot think of any man
I *truly* loved
whose phantom child
I did not fantasise
Does this mean I'm not a feminist?

Ronke tells me
where she comes from
children belong to the mother.
This I have always known
and do not question.

So when he asks me
whether *his* son is kicking
and hopes I remember to give
his boy *his* name, I only laugh,
for I have the power to be
generous or cruel
as the spirit moves me
and today,
I feel like owning my right to play
Mother-god!

A COUNTER-PRAYER TO MAWU

(Mawu is one of the names for the Supreme female creator of the Ga
people, the original inhabitants of Accra, Ghana)

Mawu, he comes bearing gifts
real silver and gilted gold
(I search among the glitter
for the frankincense and myrrh),

bottles and booties
bibs and jumpers
with clown and rabbit faces
cool blues and yellows –
colors for his son.

Something for me?

A pretty maternity shirt
with Egyptian figures
in black and white,
a clock embossed in gold
so I should always know
that time is precious
as female virtue

A poem, hallmarked love, custom-made,
calligraphed on pink paper
with flowers on the borders
for I am his girl.

He studies the ripened belly
he hasn't seen in months
and never thought he'd see again
and says, "*You are a wicked woman,
you will cut off your nose to spite your face*",

and I agree, for it is true
I breathe much easier
without a rotting nose.

A letter for my son, I beg.
He stares blankly into the T.V. screen.
A letter for our son, I plead,
for this child has rendered me
long on patience,
short on pride.

And finally, he writes
Dear son,
first I want you to know this was your mother's bright idea...
Then he promises to love,
cherish and never abandon
and gives the child a bedtime prayer
blessing mommy and daddy
and asking Jesus to help him be a good boy
until daddy comes home...

And so, I quickly offer a counter-prayer
to you, dear Mawu, from the waters of my womb.
Do not break to swallow him up
for he is flesh of my flesh and blood.

Him I warn, *Beware*
the promises you make to children,
for children are like elephants
they forget nothing,
and forgive even less!

NIGHT BLOOMING JASMINES AND WILD SAGE

If I ramble on aimlessly
or am taciturn to a fault
though I weep like a willow
or spread joy without measure
my pendulor emotions,
are but imperfect foils
for your studied neutrality.

But my love, do not misread my joy,
nor my tears as any sign of weakness
They water the earth beneath your insouciant feet
bringing forth wild orchids to blanket your shame,
camouflage the stench of your indifference,
beseeching you to come tenderly
like soft June rain
to water me till I blossom
frangipani and hibiscus
night-blooming jasmines and wild sage
to calm your restless senses,
lure your gadding heart home.

INCANTATIONS

GATEKEEPER

Meet me where the four roads cross
where all paths open, close at your whim
Meet me at the crossing
where little feet dance the fates of kings
and small axes fell giant oaks and cypresses
Meet me inbetween the cycles of seasons
dancing in time to the beat of hearts and heads

Spirit knows the road
before and after
beyond what can be seen,
so meet me at the crossroads
where blood and fire lick the knife's blade
and it doesn't matter who eats first
as long as everyone gets fed
and no bread's wasted,
while somewhere there's a hungry-belly child.

Meet me in the clearing at twilight
when night eclipses day
and fates give way to faith
Meet me twixt tomorrow,
yesterday and today

MAMA WATER

Mama water,
protector of women
riding a blue crested wave
your flouncing tail
thrashes the surface of the ocean
raising a cooling spray
to water the wills of frail
failing human spirits.

Mama water,
river mummah, Yemanja
mother-goddess, nurturer,
protector of children, fishermen
washerwomen, mothers
and would-be mothers,
accept with grace these offerings
accept with grace these salted tears
we women give back
in gratitude.

FAITH-WORKS

(To my sister Claudia May)

To be born again, made new...
to begin a new journey
where pain no longer drives me
like a cruel slave-master
to begin a-new, releasing old fears
to the kind expanse of blue
beckoning, beguiling, teasing me home
to start over, sweep the table clean of debris
to write myself a new day.

Aaaaah, release
sweet like the milk of season's first star-apple
heart keening home
leaving behind old hurts,
murky years encrusted by betrayals
mangled loved ones clawing at my veins
stretching them thin to breakage.

To begin a-new, in this new day
lovingly releasing
my fears to the eternal Spirit
who beckons, open-palmed
offering trust, faith, redemption, acceptance,
forgiveness and healing
promising to deliver to each
according to his own preparedness,
her own ability to believe,
Faith-works.

To be born a-new, this day
immersed in the power-giving light
of Grace and Good and God
spirit shining, calming me home

claiming entrance into a new way
gleaning space for light,
birthing new beginnings
accepting no conditions, greeting sunrise
with equilibrium, peaceful anticipation
to be born a-new, made over
in the image of all that is named
possible!

THE BLESSING

At the edge of night,
precipice of despair, it came:
light,
a benediction,
breaking new like dawn,
diffusing the cobwebs
splintering darkness;
light, soothing, healing,
like lilacs at twilight,
forgiving, sustaining, redemptive,
streaking magenta promises across an expanse of eternal blue;
light, healing, penetrating
warm as tamarind-leaf bath-water,
aromatic, amniotic, streaming in slow, steady;
light, energy-giving, life-sustaining,
light of Good and Truth
springing eternal like God's promise
to fill my cup until it overflows with blessings.

IS A TING ONLY A DEEP BELLY BAWL COULD EXPRESS

Losing you, Barbara, is not a ting to talk
to just any and any body about
Talking bout it only mek mi throat close up
mek de scream inside me head get so loud
is like me gaawn def.

Losing you is a ting dat only a deep belly bawl,
like what you would hear coming from a dead-yard
way up somewhere in de bush, could express,
or maybe a loud, unlady-like suck teeth
at the unfairness of dis ting call life.

But den again, maybe you gaawn
so yuh can finish wat yuh start
in a place whe no baddy no put up
no truck load a obstacle and bodderation.
Maybe yuh gaawn fe go rest up
fe a second comin'?

An when de sea-breeze blow some time
an me neck-back feel a lickle chill
a can feel yuh still, an a know yuh de bout
jus a smile pretty, wid you braids pulled back offa yuh face
an what a want to know is: Who de braid yuh hair now?
and ah hope she ain' trying to rip you off
'cause she see yuh house looking rich wid plants,
and paintings, and carvings and all dem pretty tings
yuh keep round yuh, tho' none match yuh own beautiful self.

An she betta do a good job too,
ef she know wat good fe she
'cause yuh still got nuff people fe dazzle,
enlighten and shake up, so dem can move
fe do dem own wuk, just like yuh show we,

we yuh students wat lef back yah so a try keep on nuh,
each a we doing fe we lickle piece
and knowing de standard yuh set is so high
just mek we try a lickle harder!

All fe dat...
losing the physical you of you, Barbara, is a hard ting
a ting dat only a deep belly bawl
like what you would hear coming from a dead-yard,
or maybe a balm-yard way up in de St. Thomas bush
could a ever really, really express!

*In memory of late literary critic Dr. Barbara Christian, beloved
mentor and friend.

CALL HER NANA BUUKU

(for Opal in sisterhood)

Call her Nana Buuku,
Grand Ancestress of powerful deities
call her Lickle-bit & Tallawah
call her Fire Kette
call her by her true-true name
call her by all her names
she plenty, plenty woman.

Dis woman mold words into a sacrament
brand dem on the tongues of her children
and my children and yours
to last like a benediction
from generation to generation.
Like the Spider-grandmother
she weaves words
and wisdom into a healing quilt,
wraps dem round de soul-dead
bodies of crack-heads
to warm dem back to life again.

Dis woman don't play wid words
she's a wordsmith
she know words can burn, can build,
can hide, protect, heal, reveal
secrets of the blood-bought present
the uncharted future
watch weak hearts quake
from her tongue
lashing.

Dis woman been thru de burning bush
but did not burn,
she come out tough, like tempered steel

she come out juggling fire
on de tips of all her tongues
spinning multiple languages
like a wrap-head sister
jumping in de spirit of the word
speaking tongues of flames
that consume evil-doers
dancing deliverance into every life she touches.

But touch she and you burn,
turn back to dust right before your very eyes.
You betta watch out
don't touch de Fire Kette,
don't test her tongue,
you gwine burn!

Dis woman fight the one-eyed giants with pure words
She gathering truth lickle by lickle
till dem form a wicked stone heap.
Soon she build a mountain, big like Golgotha,
but she don't turn de other cheek,
just bide her time and lie in ambush
like Granny Nanny
creating alarm in de enemy camp.

Truth has it Nanny was a deep
Cock-Pit country woman,
lickle-bit and tallawah like my sistah
a queen-mother and a down-to-earth yardie
could fend fe herself,
could fetch her own water from the river
katta roll up tight, gourdie sitting straight pon head-top
hips asway from side to side
backside a roll, every step a dance
and never spilling a drop a water.

Truth has it Nanny was a warrior, a healer,
and a madda-woman, queen of the de balm yard
daughter of Oya and Ogun,
could wield machete and lightning
with the same magic
God-child of Yemeya,
mother of the balm-yard
decked out in Shango's colors
healing the village from its
bitter-cassava afflictions.

She would sing till Golgotha itself crumble to dust:

Mother dis great stone got to move
Mother dis great stone
Dis stone of Babylon
Mother dis great stone got to move...

And would move it too, just so!

Dis woman is a true daughter of Nanny
a leader, fierce, loving, powerful,
a fighter and a healer
she so hot, she put fire to shame,
so sweet, she mek honey want to change its name
(mine you vex Osun, wid you sexy sassiness)
Dis woman can read your whole life,
and give you the words to fix what's broken
Dis woman is bigger dan the sum of all her parts
she coming to you straight, live and direct
like Shango lightning arrow,
hot, hot, hot, like a real Fire Kette
when she a burning down Babylon.
But her healing touch is righteous,
cool, like a long drink of coconut water
after a hot day digging haffu yams in the sun,

Hear her sing till Golgotha itself crumble to dust:

Mother dis great stone got to move
Mother dis great stone
Dis stone of Babylon
Mother dis great stone got to move...

And she move it too, just so!

So call her Fire Kette
call her Nana Buuku
Call her Lickle-bit and Tallawah
Call her Opal Palmer Adisa,
but call her,
cause she woman
she plenty, plenty 'oman.

OMO ANYAN

This young man
used to be a real son-of-a-gun,
such a blood-letting,
grudge-bearing, angry young 'un
quick to shoot off
mouth
gun
cum
without discretion,
such a son-of-a-gun was he.

Till de drums ketch him.

One night Omo Gun was just passing by
a balm-yard; him smell the burning gun-
powder sweet, sweet in the night air,
hear de drums beating out a steady
ruk-kum-ku-kum, a ruck-kum ku kum
a rata a tata rata tata du dum du dum
du dum du dum.
Beat get to him head
Him head start crawl wid all kinda image:
serpent making love to de rainbow,
and earth, sky, tree, dog, bird, man,
blood bending down
to de god of too many names.

Mind ketch a-fire
Him run past de healer
knock down the bottle lamp
reaching fah de coconut water
fe cool down him head
'fore him know it,
somebaddy spin him,

anodder one turn him roll
till him dancing in the center
spinning out of control.

Him nevah lef de balm yard.

Now him is a real son of the drum!
Every night him beating out rhythm
to ketch some poor lost soul
like him old self
before de drum rub-a-dub him
wid a ruk-kum-ku-kum, a ruck-kum ku kum
a rata a tata rata tata du dum du dum
du dum du dum
now him is a bonafide Omo Anyan,
son of de drum!

GOOD KEEPS

For everything there is a season,
and this is a season of waiting.

In another life I believed that good things were too fleeting,
now I know that only bad times do not last.
Good keeps, surprises you at unexpected moments,
like suddenly remembering
the high-yellow Auntie on your father's side
whose girls are the spitting image of your daughter
and being able to have you confirm the truth of it.

My brother, my heart
my love for you stays constant
though seasons change,
and change again.

I will wait for you right here by the banks of this canal
watch the fish jump, listen to my children shriek
as they chase butterflies from the patch of wild flowers
I have purposefully allowed to grow – weeds in my neighbor's yard,
she mows them down aggressively every fourth night.

But if I can carve out circles for purple wild flowers
mow around them for the butterflies' sakes
as well as for my own – because I need butterflies,
and the sound of children shrieking,
just as surely as I need you free –
then I can also sit here and wait for you

Knowing that one day
we will sit somewhere together,
and feel the sun warming our thighs
and watch the fish jump
and listen to the children,

grown bigger then,
shriek in different voices
chasing other fleeting things.

You and I
we will sit there together
on the banks of some river
beyond need for words
and be free.

FIRST RAIN

I name you
First Rain
like this poem
coming hard, fast
driving need away.

First Rain,
luminous, iconoclastic
shattering the illusions of everlasting dryness
relieving the parchedness of throats
and hallowed fields...
promising a harvest of hope,
truth unvarnished.

Though deluges may follow
the first rain that breaks the drought
is the most welcome.

AGAINST ALL LAWS

Softly,
you come to me
and i bloom you
wild orchids out of season
red hibiscus in white,
bitter, new york winter

now that I am perpetually in bloom
i will forever flower for you
'gainst all the laws of nature.

RAIN MAN
(for my husband, Cush)

1

Here I stand,
thirsty with need
Rain man, come rain in me,
water me till I am quenched.

2

Tonight it will rain...
The fresh green
scent of coming showers pervades the air,
you can almost hear it humming in the distance,
a soft sweet breeze carrying
moistness to the back of your neck,
just above your upper lip
underneath your armpits.
You can taste it on your tongue
the sweet sugarcane bite of it,
a promise of lush
dark green foliage and
fruitful harvests.

3

Tonight it will rain
and you will come to me
your blue cotton shirt
dampened from the drizzle
Just a light spattering,
you will say, and I will smile
and brush the raindrops from your locks
kiss the dewy wetness

of your beard and moustache
till you turn eagerly and find my lips
soft, dark and smooth like Dragon Stout
enough to get you mellow,
but never drunk...

4

Tonight it will rain, I promise
And you will come into me
your tongue testing,
tasting
teasing
my nipples taut and erect
your work-rough hands cupping my breasts,
round and firm like sweetie mangoes
and I will grow fertile and yielding
like a fallow field bursting with the urge
to grow new things...

5

Tonight, my cool dark man, it will rain
And we will make moisture enough
to smooth out all your rough edges
I will guide you inside me
direct the gentle thrusting of your hips
till you move faster
in sync with the rhythm of my pulse.
You and me together, loving real good,
the pitter-patter of your heartbeat echoing
the sound of raindrops on my zinc roof
love's first and best music
pitter, patter, pitter, patter
pitter, patter, pitter, patter....

6

Tonight
I will call down the rain
evoke your presence here with me
to water this seed of passion
I've been nurturing for so long
this earthy, unadorned
love jones, I carry
just for you, my Rain Making Man
just for you.

COME IN

Oh, to be young again
to grind the night away on the dance floor
return to tango in torrid sheets
or lose ourselves en route
to golden gates
of passionate promises
and find our soul's redemption in
one innocent kiss...

Such sentimental foolishness
keeps ideals alive

Youth renews its vigor
beckoning the heart
to come in from the
godless cold.

CALLALOO FOR AUDRE

(for Audre Lorde, whose spirit lives on)

From you I learned that a love
that risked nothing
wasn't worth the having.

There's a peach from Myrna nestled
in tissue paper in my handbag,
while a tenderhearted Trini
makes you callaloo and crab
in my cozy Harlem kitchenette.
The aroma of hot peppers, spinach and ochroes
simmered down with crab legs and oysters
will make Lenox Hill Hospital smell like
Gloria's kitchen in St. Croix.

I wasn't prepared for the look of acceptance,
but your indignation over losing your locks
lit that old spark that was surely you.

My gifts to Oshun couldn't save you,
but the blessing of your hand
on my early glowing
has brightened into a twelve year old beauty of a boy
who makes the question you used to ask me
("How will you use it?")
the defining query of this
spirit-charted journey.

CHATTER-BOX

(for my red-headed sister, and co-mother, Pepper Black)

Because I am not a keeper
of my own secrets
does not mean I will not guard yours
in my grandmother's thread bag
that I inherited and keep close to my heart.
It is just that I am a poet
and poets come in only two kinds:
mad truth-seekers or prophets
It is often hard to tell them apart.

Because I am not a keeper
of my own secrets
does not mean I will not carry yours to the grave
it is just that I am a storyteller
and truth is always more fantastic than fiction.
Or maybe it is because
I believe in nursing babies,
not pain.

AFTERWORD

In the offices of full disclosure and transparency, I must confess I came to the cultural expressivity of the West Indies by way of Harry Belafonte. This is the shocking truth of the matter. When I first heard his melodic voice singing of working "all night on a drink of rum," and traveling "down the way where the nights are gay," I was bowled over. At the time I did not even realize it was the rhythm and beat and heart sounds of love and labor from an ocean place I didn't know that had hooked me. I remember playing Belafonte for two of my pubescent African-American buddies, hearing them laugh and say: "Can we put LaVern Baker (ne: Delores Williams) back on now, Houston?" *Jim Dandy to the rescue!* Within a few months, Belafonte was topping the charts and everyone was calling: "Come mister tally man, tally me banana."

I have no reliable genealogy for the modern emergence of these Caribbean heart sounds and spirit rhythms of hard-day's nights in geographies by the sea, but I do know my own next acquaintance with the island sound was Bob Marley and the Wailers. On the advice of Roy Bryce-Laporte of Yale University I wrote to Rex Nettleford and asked if I could come to Jamaica to do research and give a lecture or two at Mona and Montego Bay. Professor Nettleford said "yes." I discovered in Jamaica Marley's *Catch A Fire,* with its hauntingly hard rhythms of "Duppy Conqueror" and "Small Axe" – and Rex took me to see Miss Louise Bennett in that year's *Pantomime*. I was escorted to *Sangster's* where I bought more books than I could possibly carry back to the States. I was all at once a fervid enthusiast of West Indian creativity. I relished the hospitality of Jamaica's then thriving Black Nationalism, as well as the lilt of the impossible-for-me-to-comprehend vernacular signifying of Miss Louise. There existed then a seemingly invincible credo, archive, poetry, and music of a brave new world blowing into existence. Of course, when I carefully transported my copy of *Catch A Fire* to a party that numbered on its guest list a few citizens of the Caribbean, they were *the first stateside voices* to cry: "Put Marvin Gaye back on, man!" Go figure!

My first education in matters Caribbean was, thus, garnered far less from annals of CLR James, Frantz Fanon, and Eric Williams than from the clash – the "noise in the blood" – of West Indian popular cultural tradition, and that tradition as modified by, for example, Island Records, to appeal to what quickly became transnational taste. By the mid-1970s, I was directing an Afro-American Studies Program, reading everything Black American, African, and Caribbean I could get my hands on, and advocating fiercely for a New Black Aesthetic. Those who had known me as a sedate scholar of English Victorian Literature thought I had lost my mind, or at least my cultural instincts for academic survival and white professional approval. They were probably right.

But my interests are stubborn; once found and framed, they seldom disappear. And when I had the good fortune to become acquainted with a group of quite extraordinary creative scholars, poets, cultural critics, and diasporic activists at Florida International University a few years back, I realized that though I had absorbed and learned much in my academic journey, there were still "many rivers to cross" before I came even close to the Zion highest freedom of "reading" the Caribbean and its bounteous legacies. And it was in that moment of new acquaintances and during the commencement of our new millennium that I was first blessed by the presence and work of Professor Donna Weir-Soley. Of course since the present meditation is an "Afterword," you too are now acquainted with the work of Professor Weir-Soley. We must together, I think, give forth a single utterance at this moment of the endgame, and that would be: *Ashe*!

Divided into four mutually harmonic and rhythmic sections, the first quality one notes of Weir-Soley's striking volume is its multivariate **texture**: "In Your floral skirt and crisp round-collar white blouse, /your long boney hands crossed in your lap, /you could have been dressed for Wednesday night prayer meeting. /Grandma, your eyes held high purple St. Catherine hills, and the promise of rain water." This is an evocation so keenly fine; a single cracked photograph of Teresa Matilda McCalla McCalla becomes an entire geography, a complete ecology of cultural memory. Then there is the mythically imagined and orphaned soliloquy of an inescapable emblem of colonization – Caliban and Miranda's inevitable progeny: "Me is de outside chile / de illegitimate one / mother toss back her head / declare herself unwilling / unwitting accomplice in mi conception / declare me bastard." The imaginary at work here is one of in/corporation and in/carnation – a poetical birthing into her own *sui generis* expressivity of Weir-Soley's reading of all "pressions" of the West against the rest of us, and of our escape, in resolutely acerbic and hybrid syllables: "til I and I become de bo in bombo / eloquent and sacrilegious / yuh will love me yet! / know me / name me right / when me upset de table at yuh dinner-party / turn over de dutchie pot / off de pimento wood fire / dumpling turn to ashes / caviar nestling in vomit / say yeah, a me rule / fire an' brimstone to rass! / a weh oonuu tek dis ting fah?" What, indeed, take it for, but a "thing of darkness," one that even in Shakespearean economies Prospero must acknowledge as his own.

The memory of Weir-Soley's poetry is not nostalgia, but cultural reconstruction. The politics of her poems is not bombast or bravado, but mythically informed revelation of the dread complexities of cultural contact under the aegis of uneven development and unending servitude – whether to "social death," or to World Bank and International Monetary fund debt. Weir-Soley's expressive creative world is one in which women do cry salty tears that water the earth by oceans and bring forth new birth. It is a universe in which one's actual siblings, black men brought from the Caribbean to America, go mad, speak jigsaw and delusional mania to a world out of kilter. It is a landscape of **relationships** in which Uncle Miguel under the sign of Ogun welds multiple found parts to yield a functioning engine and a gleaming truck whose painted flames are by default the envy of the island. It is an enclave of expressed **gratitude for ancestral gifts and mentoring**: "Losing you Barbara is not a ting to talk . . . / Losing you is a ting dat only a deep belly bawl / like what you would hear coming from a dead-yard / way up in de bush somewhere could express / or maybe a loud, unlady-like suck teeth / at the unfairness of dis ting we call life." This excerpt from the poem "Is a ting only a deep belly bawl could express" is an elegiac lament for the transition of the great critic/scholar Barbara Christian. However, it is also an incantation and perpetual summoning of the grace of all our ancestral teacher/mentors. There are poems, as well, of deeply passionate, rain-soaked physical embrace in Harlem nights: "And now, here I stand / naked and whole / on a cracked harlem street / naked, so you can see / there are no razors in my bra / nor explosives under my skirt / I have no other motive / but love, though I chose you." And everywhere there are children, carrying that prescient mysticism of textured memory the English poet Wordsworth speaks of so reverentially. Of her own child: "What's in a name / they will say / difficult, exotic, different. / My son, I want you to tell them / Chenjerai means brilliant / stars lighting the stairs to the pyramids / Chenjerai means clever / Bre'r Anansi outsmarting Bre'r Fox."

Everywhere in *First Rain*, the **multiplicity and complexity** of orishas and loas – the syncretisms of "here" and "there," "now" and "then," past" and "present" – commingle in the manner of the deep hard/heart beat behind a solacing balladic voice singing: "No Woman No Cry." Working "all night" in the poems of *First Rain* signifies the menial, backbreaking, low-waged migrant labor of caring for ornery patients in assisted living facilities in the US in order to pay rent and send Yankee Dollars back to the islands. The new life promised the black body having moved from Caribbean south to American north morphs horrifically into incarceration: "at seventeen he's six feet tall/ *and black and male and threatening* / and the hungry white wolves / are howling for his blood / and Sistah love is not big enough / Sistah love is not deep enough / Sistah love is not enough-enough / to protect him!"

Like multiplicity and complexity, music is everywhere is *First Rain*. It was perhaps the volume's omnipresent musical expression of the spirit that drew me back to the youth I referenced at the outset of this meditation, and bonded me forever to the promise that resonates through the entirety of this wonderful work of art created by Donna Weir-Soley. Hers is expressivity not to be passed on (not to be missed). We must engage it in its resonant nurturing if we are ever to build our love on one diasporically local, but globally committed, foundation. Our salvation is what we have and can yet salvage from traumas of middle passage, agonies of our present tense. Donna Weir-Soley's volume is our first rain toward that salvation, and is brilliantly and aptly titled.

> I name you
> First Rain
> Like this poem
> Coming hard, fast
> Driving need away
>
> First Rain.
> Luminous, iconoclastic
> Shattering illusions of everlasting dryness
> Relieving the parch-ness of throats/
> And hallowed fields …
> Promising a harvest of hope,
> Truth unvarnished.
>
> Though deluges may follow
> The first rain that breaks the drought
> Is the most welcome.

And we all say: *Ashe!*

Houston A. Baker, Jr.
Duke University

Peepal Tree Press publishes a wide selection of outstanding fiction, poetry, drama, history and literary criticism with a focus on the Caribbean and its diaspora.

Ask for our free catalogues

Visit the Peepal Tree website and buy online at:

www.peepaltreepress.com

17 King's Avenue, Leeds LS6 1QS, United Kingdom
contact@peepaltreepress.com
tel: 44 (0)113 245 1703

Recent & forthcoming Poetry

Opal Palmer Adisa, *Caribbean Passion*, 1-900715-92-9, £7.99
Feisty, sensuous — and always thought provoking. Whether she is writing about history, family, Black lives, about love and sexual passion, there is an acute eye for the contraries of experience.

Opal Palmer Adisa, *I Name me Name: Lola*, 1-84523-044-2, £8.99
March 2007 Autobiography, dramatic monologues, lyrical observations, encomiums, prose poems and prophetic rants enact the construction of an identity that encompasses inner 'i-ness', gender, race, geography, the spiritual, the social and the political.

Jacqueline Bishop, *Fauna*, 1-84523-032-9, £7.99
Using metaphors drawn from the fauna and flora of Jamaica, these poems explore the tensions between abundance and famine, the nourishing and the poisonous in memories of a rural childhood that continues to shape the present day.

Merle Collins, *Lady in a Boat*, 1-900715-85-6, £7.99
Twenty years after the death of the Grenadian revolution, Merle Collins writes of a Caribbean adrift, amnesiac and in danger of nihilistic despair. But she also achieves a life-enhancing and consoling perspective on those griefs.

David Dabydeen, *Slave Song*, 1-84523-004-3, £7.99
Songs of frustration and defiance from African slaves and displaced Indian laborers are expressed in a harsh and lyrical Guyanese Creole far removed from contemporary English in these provocative poems. (New edition with an afterword by David Dabydeen.)

Mahadai Das, *A Leaf in His Ear: Selected Poems*, 1-900715-59-7, £8.99
May 2007 This selected poems, discussed with Mahadai Das before her death, brings together all the poems from *I Want to be a Poetess of my People*, *My Finer Steel will Grow*, *Bones* and previously uncollected poems.

Kwame Dawes, *Impossible Flying*, 1-84523-039-6, £7.99
October 2006 Dawes's most personal and universal collection in its focus on family and human suffering. The poems deal with family, focusing primarily on the triangular relationship between the poet, his father and younger brother, though there is also a deeply moving acknowledgement of the rocklike unconditionality of a mother's love and care for her family's wounded souls.

Delores Gauntlett, *The Watertank Revisited*, 1-84523-009-4, £7.99
A brother held at gunpoint, a mother paralyzed at her son's encounter with authority, and citizens in battle with the police and military are among the deeply disturbing and moving images rendered in this unflinching collection of poetry about contemporary Jamaica. The beautiful landscape and endurance of the Jamaican people are vividly described in this engaging collection from a rising Caribbean poet.

**Nicolas Guillén, *Yoruba from Cuba: Selected Poems of Nicolas Guillén*
translated by Salvador Ortiz-Carboneres 1-900715-97-X, £9.99**
This dual language selection of Cuba's most outstanding poet, Nicolás Guillén, covers the wide range of his work, in a translation that captures the colloquial vigour and incantatory rhythms of Guillén's language.

Laurence Lieberman, *Carib's Leap*, 1-84523-022-1, £12.99
Carib's Leap brings together work from a dozen previous collections, and major new poems including those on the Big Drum Dance of Carriacou, poems that are alight with almost forty years of imaginative involvement with the Caribbean.

Marina Maxwell, *Decades to Ama*, 1-84523-017-5, £9.99
These poems, which date from the 1960s to the present, include lyrical paeans to the enduring, African-born creativity of the Caribbean people, dirges for the recurrent wreckage of hopes and warrior songs against the forces of neo-colonialism and phallocentrism. In them images of destruction and regeneration vie with equal power. At the heart of a quest for an authentic Caribbean politics and culture is a journey, 'thirty-how-much years of labour in this archipelago of stones' by a woman who is truly an elemental force in Caribbean writing.

Velma Pollard, *Leaving Traces*, 1-84523-021-3, £7.99
Ranging over the Jamaican and Caribbean past and the encroachments of a turbulent world, Velma Pollard's poems return always to the quiet touchstones of love and friendship. As the middle years hurry past, her poems explore what is important, what might survive.

Raymond Ramcharitar, *American Fall*, 1-84523-043-4, £7.99
February 2007 A thoroughly individual voice, with a capacity for writing verse narratives that reverberate like the best short stories, dramatic monologues that skilfully create other voices, and lyric poems that get inside the less obvious byways of emotion.

Heather Royes, *Days and Nights of the Blue Iguana*, 1-84523-019-1, £7.99
Though they traverse the wider Caribbean and beyond, Heather Royes' centre of gravity is always Jamaica ('No exile – small sabbaticals') which arouses in her both love and exasperation. Ancestors – a nomadic family 'wandering up and down the islands', family and place are described with a painterly, compassionate eye for telling detail. The collection contains a generous selection from her first book of poems, *The Caribbean Raj*.

Dorothea Smartt, *Connecting Medium*, 1-900715-50-3, £7.99
Connecting Medium links the past to the present, the Caribbean to England, mothers to fathers. Here are poems about identity and culture, past generations and the future and a powerful sequence of poems about a black Medusa.

Rommi Smith, *Mornings and Midnights*, 1-900715-95-3, £7.99
February 2007 Rommi Smith creates the voice and world of legendary diva Gloria Silver in all her feisty sensuality. Through Gloria's journey of memory, much is said about the nature of performance and the sometimes ironic distance between the singer and the song.

Gwyneth Barber Wood, *The Garden of Forgetting*, 1-84523-007-8, £7.99
These poems explore the life-shattering loss of a father and a husband. The relationship between inner feelings and the physical environment figures prominently as the poems, written in standard English and traditional verse forms, incorporate intensely Jamaican details and metaphors.

Recent & forthcoming fiction
by women writers

Opal Palmer Adisa, *Until Judgement Comes*, 1-84523-042-6, £8.99
November 2006 Sensitive and imaginative explorations of the mystery that is the male psyche. A collection that moves the heart and head, but above all is in love with telling stories — stories within stories, the reworkings of Jamaican folktales, tall tales and myths.

Jacqueline Bishop, *The River's Song*, 1-84523-038-8, £8.99
October 2006 Jacqueline Bishop invests the coming-of-age novel with a fresh, individual quality of voice, exploring her main character's sexual awakening and growing consciousness of Jamaica's class divisions, endemic violence and the new spectre of HIV-AIDS.

Jane Bryce, *Chameleon*, 1-84523-041-8, £7.99
December 2006 Stories that explore a Nigerian childhood and adolescence and the tensions between the pleasures of being an outsider and the desire to belong. Stories that make the crossing to the Caribbean with an awareness of how much of Africa was already there.

Myriam J. A. Chancy, *The Scorpion's Claw*, 1-900715-91-0, £8.99
Set in the chaotic aftermath of the fall of Baby Doc, resistance, recovery and re-creation go to the heart of this novel, which tells the past and present of two generations of Haitians.

Marcia Douglas, *Notes from a Writer's Book of Cures and Spells*, 1-84523-016-7, £8.99
Flamingo, a young Jamaican writer, finds her life becoming enmeshed with those of her characters, and when through poverty, emigration and Jamaica's political upheavals this fictional family is dispersed, one of the characters solicits Flamingo's help to bring them back together.

Beryl Gilroy, *The Green Grass Tango*, 1-900715-47-3, £7.99
Set in a London park amongst a diverse multi-racial community of dog-walkers and bench-sitters, this is comedy about identity, ageing, loneliness, love and dogs.

Denise Harris, *In Remembrance of Her*, 1-900715-99-6, £9.99
Set in Guyana, the novel begins with a murder whose motivation seems incomprehensible. What Harris's novel reveals is a wilfully forgetful society which needs to find compassion for the restless dead if the cycle of cruelty and suffering is to be broken.

Cherie Jones, *The Burning Bush Women*, 1-900715-58-9, £8.99
In these truthtelling, strange, funny and tragic stories, set in Barbados and the USA, Cherie Jones weaves paths through the joys and suffering of women's lives, dealing with love, magic and a deep connectedness between women.

Karen King-Aribisala, *The Hangman's Game*, 1-84523-046-9, £8.99
January 2007 A slave rebellion in nineteenth century Guyana and a military dictatorship in recent Nigeria intercut and merge in unsettling ways as the characters in the historical novel-within-a novel erupt into their Caribbean author's life in Nigeria.

Alecia McKenzie, *Stories from Yard*, 1-900715-62-7, £7.99
Fear and bitterness pollute the ground from which the young female characters of these stories must struggle to grow. With many 'bad seeds' of sexual violence, lies and prejudice taking root around them, their blossoming is always under threat.

Jennifer Rahim, *Songster and Other Stories*, 1-84523-048-5, £7.99
October 2006 Rahim's stories move between the present and the past to make sense of the tensions between image and reality in contemporary Trinidad.

Ryhaan Shah, *A Silent Life*, 1-84523-002-7, £8.99
Aleyah Hassan explores the mystery that surrounds her grandmother, Nani, in this tale of cross-generational revolutionary politics. Throughout this novel, family secrets are portrayed with both social realism and poetic imagination, and themes of class, race, and gender are explored incisively.